GET THE AUDIOBOOK

jljarvis.com/pumpkins

ALSO BY J.L. JARVIS

Drake & Wilde Mysteries
Love in the Time of Pumpkins
Secrets in the Hollow
Shadow of the Horseman

Standalones
A Kiss in the Rain
App-ily Ever After
Once Upon a Winter
The Red Rose
Highland Vow

Short Stories
Seasons of Love: A Short Story Collection
The Eleventh-Hour Pact
A Christmas Yarn
The Farmer and the Belle
Work-Crush Balance

Cedar Creek
Christmas at Cedar Creek
Snowstorm at Cedar Creek
Sunlight on Cedar Creek

For more information, visit jljarvis.com.

Get monthly book news at news.jljarvis.com.

LOVE IN THE TIME OF PUMPKINS

LOVE IN THE TIME OF PUMPKINS

A SHORT STORY

DRAKE & WILDE MYSTERY
BOOK 1

J.L. JARVIS

LOVE IN THE TIME OF PUMPKINS

Published by Bookbinder Press
bookbinderpress.com

ISBN (paperback) 978-1-942767-67-1

LOVE IN THE TIME OF PUMPKINS

IRIS DRAKE ADJUSTED the collar of her 18th-century costume and stepped through the front door of the Heritage Center. The high-necked blouse and long skirt were a far cry from the smart blazers and tailored pants she once wore as a doctoral teaching assistant. But then again, everything about Sleepy Hollow was a marked departure from her old life.

"You've got this," she muttered, tucking a loose auburn curl back into her bonnet. "It's just history. *Your* history."

As she smoothed her skirt, her fingers brushed the silver Ph.D. charm on a key ring tucked deep in her pocket—a talisman she couldn't part with. It reminded her of all she had worked so hard for and all she had left behind. The memory of her dissertation defense flooded back—the panel's approving nods, their pens poised mid-note, Professor Winter's broad smile, and the thrill of knowing she stood on the precipice of something important.

Until everything unraveled.

Shaking off the thought, Iris forced herself back to the present. That part of her life was over now. Here in Sleepy Hollow, she had a chance to start fresh. Here, her passion for history would be appreciated, not appropriated.

As she approached the entrance to the Heritage Center that morning, Iris nearly bumped into Dr. Arthur Grice, the center's director. He was a tall man in his late fifties, with silver hair and an intense, hawk-like gaze. His sharp features and impeccable suits made him appear more like a stern academic than a friendly museum curator.

"Ah, Dr. Drake," he greeted her with a curt nod. "I trust you're ready for your debut as our new guide."

His tone was polite but distant, as always. Iris had never shaken the feeling that he watched her too closely, as if he had some hidden agenda behind his formal demeanor. Still, she offered a professional smile in return, pushing aside the unease.

She stepped out into the crisp October air, the autumn sunlight glinting off rooftops. Six months ago, she had been defending her dissertation on the intersection of folklore and historical events in colonial America. Today, she was about to lead her first historical tour as Sleepy Hollow's newest guide.

The town square lay ahead, awash in autumn colors and Halloween decorations. Jack-o'-lanterns grinned from every porch, their flickering candlelight casting whimsical shadows as the late afternoon deepened. A group of tourists gathered near the statue of Ichabod Crane, smartphones raised, capturing the quaint colonial architecture and vibrant fall foliage.

Iris inhaled deeply, the comforting scent of wood smoke and pumpkin spice filling the air. It transported her to childhood visits at her grandparents' log cabin, where her love for old stories and local history had taken root. That passion had driven her academic career.

Her footsteps slowed as she passed Patriot's Park, where children played tag around the André Captors' Monument, marking the spot where British spy John André was hanged. Standing amid bright autumn leaves and children's laughter, the solemn statue captured what had always fascinated Iris—the blending of past and present.

As she approached the Old Dutch Church, a vendor's cart caught her eye. The sweet scent of caramel apples and hot cider wafted through the cool air. Her stomach growled—she hadn't eaten since breakfast, too jittery about the tour.

"First tour?" the vendor asked, smiling kindly as he handed her a cup of steaming cider before she could ask.

"Is it that obvious?"

Iris smiled back, reaching for a few dollars.

The old man chuckled, waving away her money.

"You'll be fine, miss. Folks come to Sleepy Hollow for the stories. And this town? It's got stories to spare."

Iris took a sip of the cider, its warmth soothing her nerves. Encouraged, she continued toward the waiting group of tourists. The golden afternoon light bathed the historic buildings, creating a dreamlike scene. It was easy to imagine Washington Irving himself wandering these streets, gathering inspiration for his tales.

As she surveyed the crowd, Iris noted the mix of eager faces—history buffs with notebooks ready, couples on romantic getaways, families herding excited children. Her gaze lingered on a tall man in a leather jacket hurrying toward the group—a stranger with tousled dark hair and an intensity in his eyes that gave her pause.

Shaking off the distraction, Iris plastered on her best tour guide smile.

"Good evening, everyone! Welcome to Sleepy Hollow. I'm Iris Drake, and I'll be your guide through the history—and mystery—of America's most haunted village."

While they each took a turn introducing themselves, Iris let her eyes sweep over each member of the group, feeling a familiar excitement settle in. This was her chance to bring history alive in a way her research papers never could.

"Before we begin," Iris said, her voice taking on the rhythm of a storyteller. "I want you all to close your eyes for a moment and imagine. We're walking these streets over two hundred years ago, just after the Revolutionary War has ended. The air is thick with possibility... and perhaps something a little more sinister."

As the group followed her instructions, Iris indulged in a moment of satisfaction.

Yes, this is where I belong.

"Now, open your eyes," she continued softly. "Look around. Every building and every stone has a story to tell. By the end of this tour, I promise you'll never see Sleepy Hollow the same way again. Shall we begin?"

With a graceful gesture toward the Old Dutch Church, Iris led the group forward into the gathering twilight, blissfully unaware that her own story was about to take an unexpected turn.

As Iris LED the group through the historic heart of Sleepy Hollow, her earlier nerves faded, replaced by the familiar rhythm of storytelling. The tourists followed her through narrow streets and shaded paths, past colonial-era homes with weathered facades. Village buildings, brimming with centuries-old charm and eerie legends, provided the perfect backdrop for her narrative.

They arrived at the Old Dutch Church and burying ground, where rows of weathered tombstones leaned precariously under the weight of years.

Iris lowered her voice to a dramatic whisper. "See

that worn headstone there?" She gestured toward a tilted slab. "That belongs to Catriena Van Tessel, rumored to have inspired Katrina Van Tassel from Washington Irving's *The Legend of Sleepy Hollow*. Local lore says that on quiet, moonlit nights, you might still hear her laughter in the wind."

A hush fell over the group, and Iris smiled to herself, pleased with their response. There was a thrill in watching people react to history brought to life. It was this magic she had craved back in academia but had rarely found.

As they left the graveyard, Iris wove facts and folklore together, guiding them toward Philipsburg Manor. The grand estate loomed ahead, its whitewashed stone exterior stark against the deepening twilight.

"The Philips family," Iris explained, "was one of the wealthiest in colonial New York. But wealth often came at a price. This estate was worked by enslaved Africans, and some say the restless spirits of those who toiled here still wander the grounds."

She was about to elaborate when a rustling in the bushes startled the group. A dog darted out, followed by a ripple of nervous laughter. Iris couldn't resist stealing a glance at the tall man who had arrived late—Jackson Wilde. Unlike the others, he hadn't been startled, just amused. His dark eyes, however, held a skeptical look that made her brace for more.

They moved on toward the old mill, where the steady hum of the Pocantico River filled the air.

Iris continued, "This mill played a crucial role in the local economy. But during the Revolutionary War, it served another purpose—patriots ground gunpowder here for the colonial forces."

Just as Iris was about to delve into more details, Jackson interrupted, his voice low but deliberate. "Assuming, of course, Washington Irving's accounts are more than cleverly disguised fiction."

Iris turned to face him. Up close, she noticed the fine lines around his eyes, the slight stubble on his jaw, and the worn leather satchel slung over his shoulder—a satchel that looked like it had seen as many historical sites as its owner. There was a challenge in his eyes, one she recognized instantly.

"Irving may have taken creative liberties," Iris replied calmly, "but his stories often had roots in actual events and local eyewitness accounts."

Jackson raised an eyebrow. "Eyewitness accounts of headless horsemen?"

A few chuckles spread through the group, but Iris wasn't about to be outdone. "The headless horseman may be a legend, but the fear and uncertainty of life in a war-torn colony? That was very real."

Satisfied with her response, Iris continued leading the group, though she became acutely aware of Jackson's presence. He lingered at the edge of the tour, always observing, always questioning. His pointed inquiries weren't meant to disrupt, she realized, but to test her knowledge. And though it was frustrating, it was also intriguing.

At the town square, where an old Revolutionary War cannon stood proudly on display, the man's voice cut in again. "This cannon looks more ornamental than practical. The real defense would have been closer to the Hudson, no?"

Iris suppressed a smile, impressed despite herself. "Yes. This piece was placed here as a memorial after the war. But during the conflict, Sleepy Hollow saw its share of action. In fact..."

She launched into a story about a midnight raid on British troops, the group hanging on every word.

Jackson watched her closely as she spoke, his expression a mix of admiration and something else— something that sent an unexpected thrill through Iris. His challenge had shifted from skepticism to a different kind of tension, one she couldn't ignore.

The tour culminated at the bridge where, according to Irving, Ichabod Crane's fateful encounter with the headless horseman took place. The sun had long since dipped below the horizon, casting the sky in deep purples and oranges as Iris brought the group to a halt.

"Imagine," Iris began, "a crisp autumn night like this one. A schoolmaster on a weary horse, riding home through the dark, when suddenly—"

She let her voice rise and fall as she painted the scene, drawing the tourists into the eerie world of Sleepy Hollow's most famous legend. They listened intently, gasping at the right moments, their eyes wide as she described Ichabod's desperate flight across the bridge.

Even Jackson seemed captivated, though Iris caught the subtle roll of his eyes when she mentioned the pumpkin projectile that supposedly unseated Ichabod Crane.

As the story ended and the group dispersed, chattering excitedly among themselves, Iris watched them as her mind ran through the day's events. She was turning to leave when a shadow crossed her path. She looked up to find Jackson standing before her, hands casually tucked into his jacket pockets.

"Interesting tour," he said, his tone unreadable. "I'm Jackson Wilde, by the way."

"Yes, I remember."

The name clicked. She had read some of his papers back in graduate school—controversial theories on coded messages in colonial-era documents. It wasn't exactly mainstream scholarship, but it was undeniably intriguing.

"Iris Drake," she replied, straightening up. "So, Professor Wilde, I take it you're not a fan of local legends?"

A spark of amusement lit his eyes. "I prefer my history a little less... embellished. But I must admit, you're an interesting storyteller."

"History is a story," Iris countered, sensing the familiar rise of academic debate. "One pieced together from facts, yes, but also from the stories people tell and the traditions they pass down."

"Facts should stand on their own," Jackson replied,

his voice steady. "Mixing them with unverified folklore only muddies the waters of historical understanding."

Iris felt her temper rise, though she kept her tone even. "And ignoring cultural context strips history of its humanity. These 'unverified' stories often preserve truths that official records overlook."

The tension between them thickened as the cool night air crackled with unspoken challenge. Iris couldn't help but notice the way Jackson's gaze flickered, first to her eyes, then to her raised chin, as though reassessing her.

After a beat, Jackson chuckled. "Well, Ms. Drake, it seems we have quite different approaches to history. In any event, perhaps our paths will cross again."

With that, he turned and walked away, leaving Iris standing in the cool night air, watching him disappear into the shadows.

Don't be too sure.

A mix of frustration and curiosity swirled in her chest.

A soft clattering sound drew her attention, like the faint clop of hooves on cobblestones. Iris turned sharply, but the street behind her was empty, save for the flickering shadows cast by the town's streetlamps.

Just the wind.

She ignored the shiver that ran down her spine. But in a town like Sleepy Hollow, where the line between history and legend blurred so easily, Iris wasn't sure anymore.

THE NEXT MORNING, Iris arrived at the Heritage Center, her thoughts still swirling from the previous evening. As she stepped into the quiet foyer of the beautifully restored 19th-century mansion, her mind replayed her exchange with Jackson Wilde. His pointed questions and the challenge in his eyes had irritated her yet left her intrigued. She had stayed up late reading one of his papers on Revolutionary War-era codes, begrudgingly impressed by his work.

The faint sound of footsteps on the hardwood floors pulled her from her thoughts. She made her way down the hallway toward her office, glancing at the framed historical prints lining the walls. Her small corner office, tucked away in the east wing, had a window overlooking the gardens. It was quiet there—too quiet for someone used to the lively debates and camaraderie of academic life.

"Iris?" her boss, Margaret, called from the conference room adjoining her office. "Can I see you for a moment?"

Iris stepped into the room and stopped short when she saw Jackson lounging in one of the visitor chairs, casually flipping through a historical pamphlet. He glanced up as she entered, that same half-smile that tugged at the corner of his mouth.

"Ah, Ms. Drake. Good to see you again."

Margaret, oblivious to the tension between them, beamed as she cordially corrected him. "Dr. Drake. So,

I see you two have already met. Iris, Professor Wilde is here for an important research project, and I've offered him our full cooperation."

Iris's stomach dropped. "Oh?" she repeated, her voice carefully neutral.

"Yes," Margaret continued, her excitement palpable. "In fact, I think you'd be the perfect person to assist him directly. Your knowledge of local history and folklore could be invaluable."

Jackson raised an eyebrow, his tone laced with humor as he replied, "I'm sure Dr. Drake's storytelling abilities will keep things... interesting."

Iris bit back a retort, feeling the spark of challenge in his words. She shot him a look that said *you don't know what you're in for.* She glanced away, looked at Margaret, and then forced herself to look back.

Jackson narrowed his eyes and stared into the distance. "Iris Drake... I read your dissertation on the intersection of folklore and historical events in colonial America. Fascinating work, especially your analysis of Revolutionary War folklore." He paused. "Though some of your conclusions parallel Thomas Bennett's book rather closely."

The silver Ph.D. charm burned in her pocket. Of course he'd mention Bennett's book—published three months before she defended, somehow incorporating two years of her original research. But Bennett had tenure at Yale, connections in publishing, and most importantly, a Y chromosome. She'd never been able to prove anything.

"Parallel conclusions can happen in academia," she said, keeping her voice neutral. Six months later, she still rehearsed better responses in the shower.

Jackson studied her for a moment. "Your conclusions went further than his, though. The connections you drew between military legends and secret societies —that was original work."

Something in his tone suggested he understood more than he was saying. But Iris had learned the hard way not to trust academic allies, no matter how perceptive they seemed. "The best research doesn't always happen in university libraries, Professor Wilde."

"Jackson," he corrected, then added with a scholar's precision, "And sometimes the most valuable texts hide in plain sight—like the truth behind Irving's tales."

The idea intrigued her, but she couldn't quite make out whether it was a serious thought or a subtle jab at her interest in historical folklore. So, she took the safe route and changed the subject. "This project of yours, what is it exactly?"

"I believe Washington Irving's stories—particularly *The Legend of Sleepy Hollow*—contain coded messages related to hidden Revolutionary War artifacts. These artifacts could reshape our understanding of colonial America."

Iris leaned in, still skeptical yet curious. "But Irving was just a child by the time the Revolutionary War ended. Why would he have any knowledge of war secrets, let alone encode them?"

Jackson smirked, his eyes glinting with excitement.

"Good question. Irving's family had close ties to influential figures in New York. Some Revolutionary War veterans were even friends of his parents. He could have been told stories or... hints that never made it into the official records."

Iris felt a surge of understanding. "So, Irving could have woven these stories into his work, maybe even hiding the truth behind the fiction to protect those he cared about—or those they served." Her gaze sharpened. "And who better to disguise secrets than the father of the American ghost story?"

Jackson nodded, impressed. "Exactly. It's like a legend within a legend, hiding in plain sight."

A mix of skepticism and curiosity bubbled up inside her. "That's... quite a theory."

"It's more than a theory," Jackson said, standing up and pulling a worn folder from his leather satchel. He spread several photocopies across the conference table —old letters, maps with cryptic notations, and fragments of what looked like codes.

"Take this," he said, pointing to one letter in particular. "It's correspondence between Irving and a known Revolutionary War veteran. The language is oddly formal, almost too careful. But if you apply this cipher." He overlaid a grid on the letter. "A hidden message appears."

Iris leaned in, intrigued despite herself. The hidden message was fragmented but clear—words like *secret, artifact,* and *guardian* jumped out at her. She couldn't help the flutter of excitement rising in her chest.

"I've traced similar patterns in several of Irving's works," Jackson continued, his voice quickening with enthusiasm. "The references often coincide with historical events or locations in the Hudson Valley. But I need someone who knows Irving's work—and the history of Sleepy Hollow—inside and out. Apparently, that's you."

Their eyes met, and a spark arced between them.

Before Iris could respond, Margaret clapped her hands together, clearly thrilled by the prospect.

"Perfect! I'll leave you two to it. Iris, feel free to use the conference room as long as you need."

As Margaret left the room, the door clicked shut behind her, and Iris found herself alone with Jackson. She crossed her arms, meeting his gaze evenly.

"I suppose we should establish some ground rules," Iris said, her voice steady. "Rule number one: We don't dismiss any potential sources of information—even if that source happens to be folklore or legend."

Jackson smirked but nodded. "Fair enough. Rule number two: We prioritize verifiable facts."

Iris gave a firm nod. "I have no problem with that. Rule three: we keep an open mind."

With a glint in his eyes and a reluctant smile tugging at his lips, he said, "Deal."

"Good. Now, where do we start?"

Jackson pulled more documents from his satchel, spreading them across the table in the small, book-lined room. The scent of old paper filled the air as they settled in. Acutely aware of his presence, Iris couldn't ignore the sensation when Jackson's arm brushed against hers as they pored over the documents or the faint scent of leather and cologne that lingered near him.

"So," Iris asked, focusing on a map of Sleepy Hollow from the 1780s, "what made you focus on Irving? There are more obvious choices for Revolutionary War secrets."

Jackson ran a hand through his hair, a gesture Iris was already beginning to recognize as a sign of zeal for his work.

"Irving's perfect. He was born right after the war and grew up hearing stories from veterans. And he had connections to several prominent families with Revolutionary War ties."

Iris leaned over the map. "Plus, his stories are so entrenched in local lore that any hidden messages would be disguised perfectly."

"Exactly," Jackson said, his eyes meeting hers, a moment of shared enthusiasm sparking between them.

As they worked side by side, Iris found herself reevaluating her initial impression of Jackson. His passion for uncovering history matched her own, although his methods and theories were unconventional. There was no denying the thrill of collaborating with someone who could keep pace with her curiosity and depth of knowledge.

"Look at this," Iris said, pointing to a passage in one of Irving's letters. "He mentions a 'midnight ride' to deliver 'precious cargo' to a 'friend in the hollow.' The date lines up with a known British movement up the Hudson."

Jackson leaned in, their faces close as he read over her shoulder. His breath was warm on her cheek as he murmured, "Good catch. And the route he describes doesn't match the main roads of the time. Could be a coded reference to a hidden path."

Their excitement built as the hours passed, theories forming and being discarded, debates flaring and subsiding. Slowly, a clearer picture of a secret network operating in the Hudson Valley during the Revolutionary War began to emerge.

As the clock neared nine, Iris sat back, rubbing her tired eyes. "I hate to admit it, but I think you might actually be onto something."

Jackson grinned, and that boyish expression transformed his usually serious face. "High praise, Dr. Drake. And please, call me Jackson."

"Iris," she replied, surprised at how easily the words slipped out.

As they gathered their notes, their hands brushed briefly. Iris felt a jolt of awareness as she glanced up, finding Jackson watching her with an unreadable expression.

The moment stretched between them, charged with possibilities. But before either could say more, a sudden crash echoed from somewhere in the building, shattering the quiet.

They both jumped, Jackson already moving toward the door. "What was that?"

Iris shook her head, her heart pounding for entirely new reasons. "It sounded like it came from the east wing."

Cautiously, they made their way down the darkened hallway, where the Heritage Center exhibits cast eerie shadows along the walls. Iris's pulse quickened as they turned a corner, and a figure darted across the far end of the corridor. Jackson started to give chase, but Iris caught his arm.

"Wait," she whispered. "There's another way around. Follow me."

She led the way through a narrow passage and emerged in the main exhibit hall just as the intruder was fumbling with the lock on a display case.

"Hey!" Jackson shouted, his voice firm. The figure startled, dropping something that clattered to the floor before bolting toward the emergency exit.

By the time Iris and Jackson reached the door, the intruder was gone. Jackson bent down to retrieve a crumpled piece of paper. He unfolded it to reveal a crude, hand-drawn map of Sleepy Hollow with several locations marked.

They exchanged a look, the same realization dawning on both of them.

Iris stared at the map. "People don't risk breaking and entering for mere folklore."

Jackson shook his head, a wry smile forming. "No, they don't."

As they stood in the dimly lit hall, surrounded by remnants of the past and the promise of secrets yet to be uncovered, Iris felt a shiver of uneasiness. "It's an old Bible. It's probably worth enough money to sell for drugs."

Jackson looked doubtful. "So... a random drug addict broke in to steal an old Bible to pawn for drugs? That seems oddly specific."

Feeling defensive, Iris said, "Art thefts happen all the time—well, maybe not all the time. Still, why should a museum be any different?"

Jackson wrinkled his face, then gave her a professorial look he might give to a student who'd just failed an exam. "Iris, no disrespect to the Heritage Center, but this ain't the Smithsonian."

She opened her mouth to protest, but he continued.

"And if it were, even a drug addict wouldn't be desperate enough to try to steal from it. Everyone knows museums have amazing security."

She was feeling a little annoyed and didn't try to hide it. "Fine. So, he came here for the Bible."

Jackson shrugged as though there were no other possible explanation.

Iris shrugged back. "Because he's a devoutly religious thief?"

Their laughter diffused the tension that had been building between them. But Jackson abruptly stopped laughing and bent down. "What's this?" For a moment, he stared at the map, then held it out to Iris.

"The Old Dutch Church." She studied it, then looked up, confused.

He pointed. "This mark here—under the church."

Iris leaned closer. "Hard to say. It could just be a stray mark. Or..."

"Or?" He lifted his eyebrows expectantly.

"Or—" She shot him a look as the realization struck her. "Or something under the church!"

Jackson nodded in agreement.

THE HERITAGE CENTER seemed more ominous after hours as darkness settled. Shadows stretched across the floor, deepening between the displays of colonial artifacts and Revolutionary War memorabilia.

After the police left, Iris and Jackson returned to the conference room, determined to find something in his research to verify their suspicion that the break-in was no random occurrence. They were convinced it had something to do with the church.

Hours later, they were hunched over old letters and maps, cross-referencing everything with historical accounts. The warm glow of the desk lamps illuminated their faces, but even the dim lighting couldn't hide the frustration beginning to creep in.

Iris rubbed her eyes, exhaustion weighing on her. The adrenaline from the break-in had long since faded, replaced by the quiet shuffle of papers like pieces in a puzzle they were trying to solve. Still, the excitement lingered beneath the surface, keeping her on edge.

Jackson groaned and leaned back in his chair, running a hand through his hair, leaving it slightly tousled. "We're missing something," he murmured, glancing at Iris, who sat beside him, engrossed in an old document. "These ciphers are leading us in circles." He leafed through yet another book on the Revolutionary War, the yellowed pages crackling under his fingertips.

Iris stood to stretch her legs. "Maybe we're approaching it wrong. There's so much emphasis on Irving's legends, but maybe we should be looking at his family's connections in the Hudson Valley. If someone left clues for him, they might have left traces we haven't noticed."

Jackson wearily raised an eyebrow.

Ignoring his reaction, Iris paced. "Irving wasn't just a storyteller—he was a master of hiding meaning in plain sight. Maybe we're looking at the wrong clues."

Jackson leaned back, considering. "So, we shift our focus—from Irving's words to his world."

She nodded, her excitement tempered by a rare, quiet intensity. "Let's start there. If we're chasing history, let's chase the people who lived it."

Iris stopped in the doorway and stared at the display case outside, her eyes drifting over its contents. The floorboards creaked under her feet as she walked closer, the sound echoing in the otherwise quiet room. "What if the clue isn't just in his words but in the objects they reference?"

Jackson stood, intrigued. "Go on."

Iris pointed to the item in the case. "For example, Irving's family Bible. His great-niece donated it in

1955. I remember reading about it. It contains pressed flowers from Irving's travels. There might be more to it."

Their eyes met, a spark of shared interest lighting the space between them. "Which is all very interesting, except we can't get into the case to examine it."

Iris hesitated, the responsible part of her reminding her of protocol. But the historian in her, the part that had always pushed boundaries in search of the truth, said, "Well, that's not entirely true."

"What?"

She felt terribly guilty, but curiosity soon overpowered it. She winced. "I might have noticed where Margaret keeps the display keys." Seeing Jackson's face light up, she added, "But we can't just open up cases and thumb through historical books."

He leveled a withering look. "I think I know how to handle historical books." Holding up his palm as if swearing an oath, he said, "I promise not to eat a peanut butter and jelly sandwich and lick my fingers while thumbing through the Bible."

As much as she knew he was kidding, her jaw dropped at the thought, much to Jackson's amusement. "Fine. I'll go get some nitrile gloves."

A few minutes later, Iris gently set the Bible down on the table. Jackson delicately turned the pages while Iris held a UV light, scanning the text for anything unusual. The scent of old paper filled the air, but Iris was more acutely aware of how close Jackson was as they leaned over the Bible together.

"There," Iris said, her voice barely above a whisper.

Pressed between the pages of Genesis was a dried flower, its brittle petals a deep brown with age.

Jackson leaned in close, his breath warm on her cheek. "Belladonna," he murmured.

"Deadly nightshade." Iris felt a chill run down her spine, not from the flower itself, but from what it symbolized. "The plant's associated with witchcraft and poison. But in the Revolutionary War..."

Jackson finished her thought, his eyes flickering with excitement. "Continental Army spies used it as a code name. This could be part of a larger message, hidden in plain sight."

Their faces were close—too close—and Iris's heart quickened, although not solely from the discovery. She took a step back, clearing her throat. "Let's keep looking."

They continued to examine the Bible with care. As they scanned the margins of the pages under the UV light, faint markings began to appear—so subtle that they would have been invisible to the naked eye.

Jackson leaned in closer. "Look at this," he murmured, excitement lacing his words. "It's a cipher. The symbols correspond to letters in the printed text."

Iris's heart raced as the implications hit her. "This is it. This is what we've been looking for."

For the next hour, they worked side by side, decoding the hidden message. Iris felt tension growing between them, not just in their shared enthusiasm for the discovery, but in the subtle awareness of his presence. She noticed the way Jackson furrowed his brow in concentration, the way he bit his lip as he worked. There was something intoxicating about the quiet focus they shared.

Finally, Jackson sat back, eyes gleaming. "I think I've got it."

Iris leaned in and listened intently as Jackson read aloud, "'Beneath the old church, where the horseman rides, lies the truth of our forefathers' secret guides.'"

Jackson's gaze lingered on the document, then flicked up to meet Iris's. "The timing in this message is odd. It's almost as if it aligns with British troop movements during the war, movements Irving couldn't have personally witnessed."

Iris's brow furrowed. "What if... this information wasn't originally his?" She paused, the idea growing. "Maybe Irving had access to something older—a memoir, a secret letter from someone who actually witnessed the events."

Jackson's eyes widened. "That would mean Irving wasn't creating a legend; he was passing down a hidden history." He thumbed through the document, his excitement barely contained. "That kind of document would have been priceless to a man as curious as Irving. And as the guardian of those stories, he might have felt compelled to embed them in his works."

Iris's fingers traced the edge of the map. For a moment, neither moved as the weight of the words settled over them. When Iris finally spoke, her voice came out in a whisper. "The Old Dutch Church. It must be referring to the cemetery there."

"And the horseman..." Jackson trailed off, a grin tugging at the corners of his mouth. "That has to be the bridge where your tour ended last night."

Iris shivered—not from fear, but from excitement. "It's our first real clue."

Neither of them seemed to notice how closely they'd moved toward each other. Iris took in the flecks of gold in Jackson's hazel eyes and the way his breath seemed to catch just for a moment as their gazes locked. The air between them felt charged with the thrill of the mystery and the unspoken tension that had been building since their first encounter.

Jackson's gaze flickered down to her lips, and for a brief, dizzying second, Iris thought he might close the distance between them. Instead, he stepped back and ran a hand through his hair with a nervous chuckle. "Well, it's a good start."

"Yeah," Iris breathed, her heart still hammering as the moment stretched between them.

Just as Iris began to relax, a loud crash shattered the quiet, echoing through the building.

They both flinched. Jackson was already moving toward the window. "Did you hear that?"

Iris nodded, trying to shake off the lingering warmth of the moment. "It came from the back alley."

They exchanged a glance and moved cautiously toward the rear entrance. The old floorboards creaked beneath their feet, and every shadow seemed to loom larger in the dim lighting. The Heritage Center, usually a comfortable place of history and learning, now felt unsettling.

Jackson eased the door open and peered into the darkness. For a moment, there was nothing but the cool night air and the distant rustling of leaves. Then, a sudden yowl echoed as a cat darted across the alley, knocking over a trash can.

They both let out a nervous laugh. "Just a cat," Jackson muttered, shaking his head.

But as Iris moved to close the door, she froze. Across the alley, in the shadows, a figure stood watching—tall, imposing, and just on the edge of the mist rolling in. Before she could react, it dissolved into the darkness, disappearing as quickly as it had appeared.

Iris swallowed hard, her pulse quickening. "Did you see that?"

Jackson's brow furrowed. "See what?"

"Over there. Someone was watching us. I was sure..." Iris whispered, her voice tinged with unease. She glanced back at the empty alley, trying to convince herself it had just been her imagination.

Jackson's expression grew serious. "Come on, let's head back inside."

As they made their way back to the conference room, the warmth of the building felt more like a shield against the creeping disquiet that had settled over them. Iris tried to focus on the excitement of the discovery, but her thoughts kept returning to that shadowy figure in the alley. Were they being watched?

Jackson seemed to sense her unease as they

resumed their work, his voice lower, more cautious now. "We've stumbled onto something."

She met his gaze, her heart still racing. "But why now? We've just started."

Jackson's eyes darkened. "You've just started."

Iris didn't like the sound of that. "What? This isn't the first time—?"

"Strange things have happened?" he finished her thought and shook his head. "I've been at this project for months, but it wasn't until I had a breakthrough that things started to happen."

"Things?" She shut her eyes for a moment to brace herself, then looked back at him with narrowing eyes. "That might have been helpful."

He looked truly remorseful. "Iris, I'm sorry. I honestly thought I left—whatever it was—in the city."

A harsh tone crept into her voice. "Yeah, well, 'whatever it was' figured out we're a short MTA train ride away."

Jackson took her sarcasm with a nod. "I should've told you."

"You think?" Iris glared but said nothing.

"Look, there's no point in involving you in whatever this is. From here on, I'll manage myself."

Iris paused, unsure how to react. "So, you've decided all that without even letting me know what's going on?" She added bitterly, "Mr. Rule Number Two?"

To his questioning look, she added with air quotes, "We prioritize verifiable facts?"

He emitted a slight snort and practically smiled.

Iris folded her arms. "And I haven't heard one."

With a nod, Jackson exhaled. "The truth is, I don't have any facts—just the same nagging sense. A noise, a figure in the shadows—the sort of thing I talked myself out of until it happened again. And again. But when it followed me here..."

She said gently, "You should have told me."

"Told you what? That I'm imagining things that don't seem to be there?"

"Well, that burglar was there."

"Yes. Finally—something real. But the rest is out there in the ether."

Iris lifted her shoulders. "So, we'll figure it out."

"We?" Jackson shook his head. "I'm not dragging you into all this."

Iris thought about all the years she had spent chasing historical truths and how she had dreamed of one day being part of a breakthrough. With a steady gaze, she said, "I'm in if you are."

A slow smile spread across Jackson's face, something warm and admiring in his eyes. But he shook his head slowly. "I don't know..."

"Well, I do," Iris said matter-of-factly.

He didn't speak for a moment. "Well, okay."

An illogical happiness surged through her. "Okay."

Jackson lifted his eyebrows. "Then let's see where this takes us."

As they packed up their materials, a sense of urgency hung in the air. They locked up the Heritage

Center and stepped out into the misty night, where the quiet streets of Sleepy Hollow felt charged with possibility.

The fog had thickened, curling around the street-lamps and casting eerie shadows. An owl hooted in the distance, its call echoing down the deserted streets. Iris and Jackson shared a look as they walked side by side. The weight of history pressed down on her while the excitement of what lay ahead pulled her forward.

THE OLD DUTCH Church glowed with the soft light of flickering candles and jack-o'-lanterns lining the path to its ancient doors. The night air was crisp, with the scent of wood smoke and fallen leaves mingling with the faint sounds of laughter drifting from the town square. It was Halloween night, and the town had come alive with its legends.

Iris adjusted the deep burgundy gown she had borrowed from the Heritage Center's costume closet. It felt oddly appropriate, given the night's events. The rustle of the heavy fabric against her legs and the period hairstyle she had crafted made her feel as though she had stepped back in time. Beside her, Jackson cut an impressive figure in a Revolutionary War officer's uniform. The jacket might as well have been tailored to fit his broad shoulders. But his playful smirk kept him from looking too serious.

"Remember," Jackson murmured as they

approached the church, his breath warm in the cool night air, "we're just here to enjoy the gala. We don't want to draw any attention."

Iris nodded, accepting his offered arm. "Agreed. Though I still wish we could've brought the Bible with us."

"It's evidence. Too risky," Jackson replied, his eyes scanning the crowd ahead of them. "If our theory is correct, there could be others here tonight who'd rather that evidence stay hidden."

Inside, the austere church had been transformed for the evening, its usual solemnity replaced with a festive air. Faux cobwebs hung from each corner, and candlelit chandeliers cast an amber glow on the costumed guests. The room hummed with the sounds of laughter and clinking glasses. In the historical setting, the mix of colonial figures, ghosts, and goblins was a surreal contrast.

As Iris and Jackson entered, more than a few heads turned in their direction. Iris wasn't surprised. While their costumes were well-constructed period replicas, Jackson cut a handsome figure in uniform, drawing more than a few admiring looks.

"You clean up pretty well," Jackson teased.

Iris blushed. "You're not half bad yourself."

While the earlier edge between them had softened, an undercurrent of tension lingered—a shared awareness that something threatened to surface beneath Sleepy Hollow's legends, and they were closer than ever to uncovering it.

As they mingled through the crowd, Iris's gaze was drawn to the far side of the room, where Dr. Grice, the head of the Heritage Center, stood watching the festivities. His sharp eyes locked on hers, and Iris felt a flicker of unease. His attention seemed coincidental. He had been pleasant enough in their professional interactions, but now, with everything she and Jackson had uncovered, she couldn't help feeling suspicious of everyone, including Dr. Grice.

Jackson followed her gaze. "Grice is here," he muttered, his expression hardening.

"I know," Iris replied, her smile fading as she noticed Grice's calculating look. "He's watching us."

"Be careful." Before they could linger too long, Jackson steered them away, nodding toward the refreshment table. "Let's schmooze."

They made their way through the crowd, pausing every so often to exchange pleasantries with other guests. Iris noticed how easily Jackson slipped into conversation with the locals, his charm disarming even the most aloof attendees. She supposed that was one reason he was so good at his work—he had a way of getting people to open up, even when they didn't realize they were doing it.

"Did you hear about the strange lights in the cemetery last night?" a tipsy woman in a witch's hat leaned in to whisper conspiratorially as they passed. "Old man Fredericks swears it was the headless horseman. Says he's come to claim another soul!"

Jackson chuckled politely, but Iris felt him tense

beside her. They exchanged a questioning glance. Could someone have been snooping around the Old Dutch Church for reasons beyond Halloween?

As Jackson went to fetch drinks, Dr. Grice cornered Iris. His expression was unreadable as he approached, his gaze sweeping over her costume with mild interest.

"Enjoying the party?" Grice's tone was polite, but there was an edge beneath it that made her uneasy.

"It's lovely," Iris replied, forcing a smile. "The Historical Society has outdone itself."

Grice nodded, taking a slow sip from his glass. "Indeed. It's important to keep our history alive, isn't it? Though some parts of history are better left in the past, wouldn't you agree?"

Iris's smile stiffened as Grice's gaze hardened. "History," he continued, his voice low, "isn't just a story for the masses, Dr. Drake. It's a legacy—a delicate one that should remain in the right hands."

Iris clenched her hands, her voice calm but defiant. "And who decides which parts of history are worth preserving? Or who has a right to them?"

Dr. Grice's lips twisted into a cold smile. "Those who truly understand its power," he replied, his voice almost a whisper. "I spent decades protecting these secrets from people who would misuse them. Outsiders, academics—people who would tear down our heritage for the sake of discovery. You and Professor Wilde have no idea of the legacy you're meddling with."

There it was—the subtle warning in his words, as

though he knew exactly what she and Jackson had uncovered.

Iris suppressed a shiver, forcing herself to hold his gaze. "Maybe you've spent too long in the shadows, Dr Grice. Some truths are worth bringing to light."

Before Iris could go on, Jackson reappeared, smoothly inserting himself into the conversation. "Dr. Grice, it's good to see you. I've heard so much about your work here."

Grice's expression didn't change, but his eyes flicked between the two of them, sharp and calculating. "Ah, Professor Wilde. Yes, I've heard quite a bit about you as well."

Jackson smiled, though Iris could see the tension in his posture. "All good, I hope."

Grice's lips curved into a thin smile. "One can always hope." He held their gaze for a moment longer before turning away, disappearing into the crowd as swiftly as he had appeared.

"That was... unsettling," Iris muttered as soon as Grice was out of earshot.

Jackson nodded, his expression serious. "We need to move. Now."

They slipped away from the crowd and headed toward the rear of the church, where they suspected hidden passages lay. The festivities behind them faded as they moved down the church's corridors. Soon, the flickering candlelight gave way to darkness. The narrow halls echoed with the sound of their footsteps, and the ancient floorboards creaked under their weight.

Iris's heart raced, though she wasn't sure if it was from the thrill of discovery or from the tension that seemed to have grown thicker in the quiet space. As they approached the back wall, Jackson pointed to an old tapestry.

"The symbols on the border," he whispered, "match the cipher from Irving's Bible."

Iris ran her fingers along the woven edge, her pulse quickening. "There's something here." Her fingers found a small latch hidden behind the tapestry. With a quiet click, a door swung open, revealing a narrow staircase descending into darkness.

Jackson gave her a wry smile. "Ladies first?"

Iris rolled her eyes but couldn't help the grin that followed. "Age before beauty."

Cautiously, they moved down the stone steps, the air growing cooler as they descended. The passage led them to a small chamber lined with dusty shelves and filled with relics from centuries past. In the center of the room, resting on a simple wooden pedestal, was an ornate wooden box.

Iris's breath caught in her throat. "This is it. This is what we've been looking for."

Before they could investigate further, a voice came from the stairwell behind them.

"I wouldn't touch that if I were you."

They both spun around to find Dr. Grice standing in the doorway, his expression cold and his posture rigid. But it wasn't just Grice's sudden appearance that made Iris's heart drop—it was the antique pistol he held aimed directly at them.

"Dr. Grice?" Iris's voice faltered, her mind racing. "What—why?"

"I'm protecting a legacy." Grice's voice was as cold as the stone walls around them. "A legacy that must remain hidden."

Jackson stepped forward, instinctively shielding Iris. "This belongs in a museum, Dr. Grice. It's part of history."

Grice's laugh was bitter. "History? You have no idea what you're meddling with. Some things are better left buried."

As Grice's finger twitched on the trigger, Iris's eyes darted to the far wall, where something looked... wrong. Her gaze locked onto a section of stone that didn't quite match the rest, and she realized with a jolt that the wall was hollow. And all she could think of was never seeing her family upstate and the historical discovery that would never be brought to light—because her boss had a gun, and he was too close to miss.

"Now," Grice continued, his voice low, "step away from the—"

Before he could finish, Iris's hand found a small indentation in the stone. She pressed it, and the wall swung open with a low groan, revealing a hidden passage.

At that moment, Jackson lunged at Grice, tackling him to the ground. The pistol went off with a deafening crack, the shot missing and hitting the ceiling, showering them in dust and stone fragments.

"Iris, go!" Jackson shouted as he wrestled the gun from Grice's grip.

Without hesitation, Iris grabbed the wooden box from the pedestal and sprinted into the hidden passage. The tunnel was narrow and dark, the walls cold against her fingertips as she raced through the twisting path. Behind her, she heard the scuffle of footsteps and glanced back to see Jackson catching up, but the sounds of pursuit were not far behind.

Iris and Jackson burst through the tunnel and into the Old Dutch cemetery, the cool night air hitting Iris's face like a shock. The sound of lively Halloween festivities was gone, replaced by the heavy stillness of the graveyard. The moon cast long shadows over the ancient headstones.

"This way!" Jackson shouted, grabbing Iris's hand as they ran toward the town.

They wove through the rows of tombstones, their footsteps crunching on fallen leaves. Iris's gown snagged on some brambles and tore, but she didn't stop. Grice's shouts echoed through the cemetery. She could only hope he was too far away to follow.

As they reached the edge of the church grounds, they collided with a group of partygoers heading home.

"Whoa!" A man dressed as Frankenstein laughed, oblivious to the tension in the air. "The haunted hayride's that way, dude!"

Iris and Jackson slipped into the remaining crowd,

blending in as they hurried down the street. They didn't dare look back.

Rounding a corner, they ducked into an alley. Panting, they pressed against the wall, catching their breath. Iris heard Jackson's deep breathing fall into sync with her own as they stood close in the darkness.

"You okay?" Jackson whispered, his voice rough.

Iris nodded, looking up at him. His cheek was smudged with dirt, a cut visible just above his eyebrow. She reached up without thinking, brushing her fingers lightly over the bruise. "You're hurt."

Jackson caught her hand and held it. "I'm fine. You're what matters."

The moment stretched between them. Iris's heart hammered in her chest, and for a brief second, she thought Jackson might lean in. She hoped he might—

A shout from the distance shattered the moment. They both jumped, the spell broken.

"We need to go," Jackson said, pulling away.

They hurried down the alley, their pace quick but quiet, the weight of the wooden box heavy in Iris's arms. As they neared the bridge at the edge of town, a cool mist rolled off the river, obscuring her vision.

A mix of relief and apprehension coursed through Iris. They'd escaped—for now. But what had they uncovered? And who else was after it?

The mystery of Sleepy Hollow was darker and more dangerous than Iris had ever imagined. But as she looked at Jackson, his uniform disheveled, his expression still sharp, Iris realized she wasn't in this alone.

IRIS AND JACKSON slowed as they reached the stone bridge shrouded in mist that clung to the riverbank. The night had grown eerily quiet as Halloween revelers headed home, and Sleepy Hollow settled into its usual stillness.

Iris leaned against the guardrail, clutching the ornate wooden box to her chest. Her heart was still racing, not just from the chase but from the weight of everything that had happened—the dark passages, Dr. Grice's betrayal, and the knowledge that they had uncovered something of a scope they still didn't fully understand.

Beside her, Jackson scanned the path behind them for signs of pursuit. His chest rose and fell with heavy breaths, but his eyes were focused, as if already planning their next move. For a moment, they were silent, the adrenaline ebbing away.

"That was..." Iris started, still trying to catch her breath.

"Yeah," Jackson agreed, his voice low as he finally relaxed against the guardrail beside her. They exchanged a look and, almost in unison, laughed—soft, breathless laughter in the aftermath of their narrow escape.

As their laughter subsided, the weight of the box in Iris's arms brought her back to the present.

"We actually found it," she said, her voice tinged with disbelief as she carefully set the box down on the railing.

Jackson's grin returned as he leaned over to inspect the box.

"It's the real thing, Iris. We just need to figure out what's inside."

His fingers traced the intricate carvings along the box's surface, symbols that mirrored the ciphers they had found in Irving's Bible.

The lock, which had seemed daunting in the hidden chamber, now opened with surprising ease.

Inside lay a bundle of letters on parchment yellowed with age. Beneath them rested a small leather-bound journal, its edges frayed but intact. Iris gently unfolded the top letter. Her eyes widened at the familiar script.

"Jackson, this is in Washington's hand," she whispered, awe creeping into her voice. "It's... to a secret society. The 'Wardens of Liberty.'"

Jackson leaned closer, his brow furrowing as he scanned the contents. "This is bigger than we thought," he murmured, flipping through the journal's pages. "Look at these names—Benjamin Franklin, John Jay, Alexander Hamilton. They weren't just founding fathers; they were part of a secret network."

His voice grew more intense as he read. "The journal entries span decades. Listen to this one from 1799. 'Our European brothers warn of strange lights in the skies above Prussia. The Crown's agents seek what they cannot understand. We must maintain our vigilance, for the fate of the new republic depends upon keeping certain truths buried.'"

Iris's pulse quickened. "The sightings—they're not just local folklore?"

"No," Jackson replied, pulling out another document. "These are systematic observations documented across continents. The Wardens weren't just protecting political secrets; they were guarding something else entirely."

A sound—low and distant—cut through the night air. The unmistakable rhythm of hooves pounded against packed earth. Through the shifting mist, a figure emerged on horseback, its outline strange and distorted in the moonlight. Where the rider's head should have been, there was nothing but shadow.

The figure charged. Jackson pulled Iris to safety as the horse thundered past, the rush of air carrying an electric charge that made the hair on their arms stand up. The scent that followed wasn't brimstone but something sharper, almost metallic.

"Did you see that?" Iris whispered, her academic mind already cataloging details. "The way it moved—it wasn't natural. And that light around it..."

"Like the aurora borealis," Jackson muttered, "but contained, controlled." They stared long after the vision was gone. Jackson shook his head and pulled another letter from the box. "Here. Coded coordinates. Dozens of them, all along the Hudson Valley, dating back centuries."

The rider appeared again at the far end of the bridge, its form flickering like heat waves off summer pavement. This time, Iris noticed something else—a faint humming, just at the edge of hearing, and a pattern of lights beneath the horse's hooves that didn't match any known technology.

"It's not a ghost," she realized. "It never was. The legends, the sightings—they were covering something else. Something the Wardens have been monitoring since the revolution."

"And Grice knows about it," Jackson added grimly. "That's why he was willing to kill for these documents. The Heritage Center isn't just preserving history; it's an observation post."

The figure vanished, leaving only the lingering hum and the smell of ozone. Jackson began sorting through more papers, his expression growing more serious with each page.

"These letters—they're not just from the revolution. There are recent ones written in the same cipher. Names we'd recognize. Politicians, military leaders, corporate CEOs. The Wardens are still active."

"And probably not happy we found this," Iris added, her mind racing. "We need to make copies and get this information somewhere safe."

"Already on it," Jackson said, pulling out his phone and typing a text. "I have a contact who can keep documents secure. But for now, we'll hang onto this box. We need to be careful. If even half of these names are current members..."

"We're dealing with people who can make us disappear," Iris finished. She picked up a photo that had fallen from the journal—a grainy image from what appeared to be the 1950s, showing similar lights over the Hudson River.

Jackson took her hand, his expression grave but determined. "This goes deeper than either of us imagined. The historical society, the local legends, the Heritage Center—it's all an elaborate front. The question is, are we really ready to pull back that curtain?"

Iris met his gaze steadily. The academic in her, the one who'd always pushed for truth no matter the cost, already knew the answer. "We can't walk away now. Whatever the Wardens are hiding, whatever Grice is involved in—people deserve to know the truth."

"It won't be safe," Jackson warned, though she could see the same determination in his eyes. "These people have been keeping secrets for centuries. They won't stop coming after these documents—or us."

"Then we'll need to be smarter," Iris replied. She pulled out her phone and began photographing documents. "And we'll need allies—media contacts, our academic connections—people we can trust with what we've found."

Jackson touched Iris's hand and cast dark eyes on hers. "No. Not yet. We don't know who we can trust, and we won't until we get a firmer grasp on what this is about."

He was right. Iris froze, overwhelmed by the implications of what they'd stumbled onto.

With a nod toward the documents, Jackson said, "One step at a time. We'll figure it out."

Wanting so to believe him, Iris drew in a shallow

breath and proceeded. As they carefully photographed and replaced each document, a plan began taking shape. They would need secure communication channels, backup locations, and some way to verify the historical authenticity of the documents without revealing their source.

The distant sound of sirens broke through the night. Iris shuddered. "That came from the Heritage Center."

Jackson's gaze sharpened. "Someone must have reported hearing shots from there."

"We need to move." Iris packed up the contents of the box, and they headed for her apartment. Once inside, she locked the door and leaned against it, her heart hammering, barely able to breathe.

Jackson pulled her close and cradled her head in his hand. "It's okay."

Iris whispered, "I know. I'm sorry."

"Sorry? For what?"

Iris lifted her chin, losing herself in his gaze. His eyes drifted down to her lips. Any words she might have said were now lost. Her heart pounded as she felt herself drawing closer.

Jackson looked away, a half-smile teasing his lips. "I'd better go... before I don't."

Iris nodded, trying to appear to agree, which, in theory, she did, but her heart had just taken flight.

Jackson said, "There's a lot going on. We don't want to complicate things."

Complicate things? Too late for that.

Jackson kissed her on the forehead, which Iris

couldn't help but find just a little dismissive.

As if flipping a switch, his tone was all business. "First thing tomorrow," he said, "we start connecting the dots. The Wardens, their European connections, whatever they've been observing all these years."

"And we find out what's really hidden beneath the Old Dutch Church," Iris added. "Those coordinates can't be coincidence."

Picking up on his mood change, Iris agreed and saw him on his way before she locked the door and silently cried to the heavens. *What just happened?*

Unable to help herself, Iris went to the window and watched until Jackson had faded from view. From her vantage point, Sleepy Hollow's familiar shapes had transformed—each shadow a potential Warden, every flickering streetlight a possible signal.

Three quick taps at her door made her pulse jump. After a quick look through the peephole, she opened the door to find Jackson slightly breathless. "I forgot something," he said, voice low and urgent.

Unsure of what he could mean, Iris said, "The documents are safe in the box with encrypted backups in the cloud."

Barely letting her finish, Jackson shook his head. "Not that." He stepped closer, his hand rising to her cheek. "This."

His kiss burned through her defenses, deep and so sure it nearly overwhelmed her. Her fingers curled into his jacket, drawing him nearer.

When they parted, he rested his forehead against

hers "Terrible timing," he murmured, thumb tracing her cheekbone. "With everything we've uncovered, Grice, the Wardens..."

"Catastrophically bad idea," she agreed, still gripping his jacket.

A soft laugh rumbled in his chest. "The worst." His expression sobered. "It is, isn't it?"

"The worst? Maybe, but..."

"Yeah." He nodded, pressed a kiss to her temple, and whispered, "Now I really should go."

It was all she could do not to tell him to stay, but maybe he had a point. They had complicated things enough as it was. So, she kissed him goodbye and resisted the urge to tighten her grip on his jacket and refuse to let go.

As she watched Jackson disappear into the night, Iris clutched her phone, which now held copies of their discovery. Somewhere in those documents lay the truth about what the Wardens of Liberty had been protecting since the nation's founding. And now, for better or worse, she and Jackson were part of that legacy.

The game was no longer about historical research or academic recognition. It was about uncovering a truth that powerful people had killed to keep hidden. The real question was—how far would they have to go to expose it?

Something caught her eye, and she turned toward the statue of the headless horseman in the median near Philipsburg Manor. A shadow darted past the statue— too quick, too fluid for natural movement. Iris kept watching. She'd spent enough time running from shadows. Now, it was time to chase them down.

Above it, a light moved across the sky. And in the strange light of the moon, the statue's form seemed to ripple like heat waves off a distant pavement. For a moment, Iris could have sworn the statue tilted ever so slightly toward her.

But surely, that was just a trick of the shadows.

Wasn't it?

THANK YOU!

THANK YOU FOR READING! If you enjoyed this book, please consider leaving a review or a rating. Your feedback on bookstore, Goodreads, and Bookbub websites helps other readers discover books they'll enjoy.

THANK YOU!

Thank you for reading! If you enjoyed this book, please consider leaving a review or a rating on Amazon or your favorite bookstore. Your feedback helps other readers discover my work.

CONTINUE THE STORY IN BOOK 2 OF THE DRAKE & WILDE MYSTERIES

In Sleepy Hollow, history doesn't rest... and neither do its secrets.

When historian Iris Drake takes a job as a tour guide in Sleepy Hollow, she expects to share tales of headless horsemen and haunted bridges. Instead, a chance encounter with the enigmatic and brilliant Professor Jackson Wilde plunges her into a centuries-old conspiracy that could rewrite American history.

As Iris and Jackson race to decode cryptic messages left by the Founding Fathers, they uncover a world of hidden chambers, shadowy societies, and a mysterious "covenant" guarded by the Wardens of Liberty. With each clue bringing them closer to the truth—and to each other—the line between ally and enemy blurs.

Their growing attraction only heightens the stakes

as they find themselves pursued by those who would keep the past buried. In a town where legend and reality intertwine, Iris must decide how much she's willing to risk for the truth... and for love.

Because in Sleepy Hollow, some secrets are worth killing for – and others might just save a nation. But in a town where nothing is as it seems, who can they trust? Dive into the mystery today!

Find out more at
jljarvis.com/secrets/

In Sleepy Hollow, history doesn't rest... and neither do its secrets.

Historian Iris Drake sought a quiet escape as a tour guide in the legendary town of Sleepy Hollow, expecting to share tales of headless horsemen and haunted bridges. But a chance encounter with the intriguing Professor Jackson Wilde thrusts her into a hidden world that could upend everything she knows about American history.

Together, they unravel cryptic messages left by the Founding Fathers, uncovering secret chambers and shadowy societies guarded by an elusive group called the Wardens. As Iris and Jackson delve deeper, each clue pulls them closer to a truth with the power to rewrite the nation's past—and jeopardize its future.

Their undeniable attraction complicates their mission. In a maze where allies turn into enemies, and myths become reality, trusting each other is their only hope for survival. But in Sleepy Hollow, where every legend has a kernel of truth, who can they really trust?

Dive into the thrilling journey through history, mystery, and romance today!

Find out more at:
jljarvis.com/secrets/

BOOK NEWS

Sign up for the J.L. Jarvis Journal for exclusive benefits,
including free books, special offers, exclusive content,
and updates on new releases: news.jljarvis.com

BOOK NEWS

Sign up for the J.L. Jarvis Journal for exclusive benefits, including free books, special offers, exclusive content, and updates on new releases: news.jljarvis.com

ALSO BY J.L. JARVIS

Waterfront Summers

(Can be read in any order)

The Cottage at Peregrine Cove

The House on Serenity Lake

Moonlight on Mariner's Bluff

Drake & Wilde Mysteries

(Reading Order)

1 Love in the Time of Pumpkins

2 Secrets in the Hollow

3 Shadow of the Horseman

Standalones

(Can be read in any order)

A Kiss in the Rain

App-ily Ever After

Once Upon a Winter

The Red Rose

Highland Vow

Short Stories

(Can be read in any order)

Seasons of Love: A Short Story Collection

The Eleventh-Hour Pact

A Christmas Yarn

The Farmer and the Belle

Work-Crush Balance

Cedar Creek

(Can be read in any order)

Christmas at Cedar Creek

Snowstorm at Cedar Creek

Sunlight on Cedar Creek

Pine Harbor

1 *Allison's Pine Harbor Summer*

2 *Evelyn's Pine Harbor Autumn*

3 *Lydia's Pine Harbor Christmas*

Holiday House

(Can be read in any order)

The Christmas Cabin

The Winter Lodge

The Lighthouse

The Christmas Castle

The Beach House

The Christmas Tree Inn

The Holiday Hideaway

Highland Passage

For more information, visit jljarvis.com.

Get monthly book news at news.jljarvis.com.

ABOUT THE AUTHOR

J.L. Jarvis is a left-handed former opera singer/teacher/lawyer who writes books. She now lives and writes on a mountaintop in upstate New York.

jljarvis.com